Samantha Seagull's Sandals

Written by Gordon Winch
Illustrated by Tony Oliver

Gareth Stevens Publishing
Milwaukee

A long time ago
there lived a young, silver gull
who wanted to be different.
Her name was Samantha.

"Why am I the same as all the other young gulls?"
she asked Hector the Hermit Crab, who was old and wise.
"The same gray bill, the same gray legs, the same gray feet.
I want to be different. I want to be different right now!"
"Ho, ho!" said Hector in a voice as deep as the ocean.
"You will be different one day. Wait and see."

3

But Samantha could not wait.
She thought and thought until she had a bright idea.
"I know what I'll do," she said to herself.
"I'll buy some shoes.
Then I will be different."

So Samantha went to a shoe store
and bought a pair of high-heeled shoes.
"How smart and how different I am,"
she said, as she stepped onto the beach.

SQUELCH!
The heels of her shoes sank deep into the sand,
and Samantha was stuck where she stood.

"Don't be a silly seagull, Samantha,"
said her friend Simon, as he helped her out.
"I like you as you are.
You are the most beautiful seagull
in the whole wide world.
That's different enough for me."

7

The other seagulls laughed and laughed,
and Samantha felt embarrassed —
so embarrassed, in fact,
that she started to blush.
And her bill went red,
the rings around her eyes went red,
her legs and feet went red,
and she flew back to the shoe store
with her shoes to change them.

SLOSH!
Her second try at being different
was no better than her first.

Samantha's rubber boots filled with water,
and she started to sink.
"Save me, Simon. Save me!" she cried.

The other seagulls laughed and laughed,
and Samantha felt embarrassed —
so embarrassed, in fact,
that she started to blush.
And her bill went red,
the rings around her eyes went red,
her legs and feet went red,
and she flew back to the shoe store
with her rubber boots to change them.

Then Samantha bought a pair of slippers
with purple pom-poms.
They looked very warm and cozy.
"How smart and how different I will be," she said.

SPLASH!
A wave washed over her slippers
and made them wet and soggy.
Simon shook his head in dismay.

"I do wish you would stop trying to be different," said Simon.
"Everyone is laughing at you."
But Samantha was determined to be different,
and she flew back to the shoe store
with her slippers to change them.

16

17

So Samantha bought some sandals,
and she wore them all the time.
They seemed to be just the thing.
They didn't sink into the sand.
They didn't fill up with water.
And they didn't get wet and soggy.

Samantha felt so different and so pleased
with herself that she walked about
with her head held high in the air.
She didn't speak to the other seagulls.
She didn't even speak to Simon.
And Simon was sad.

19

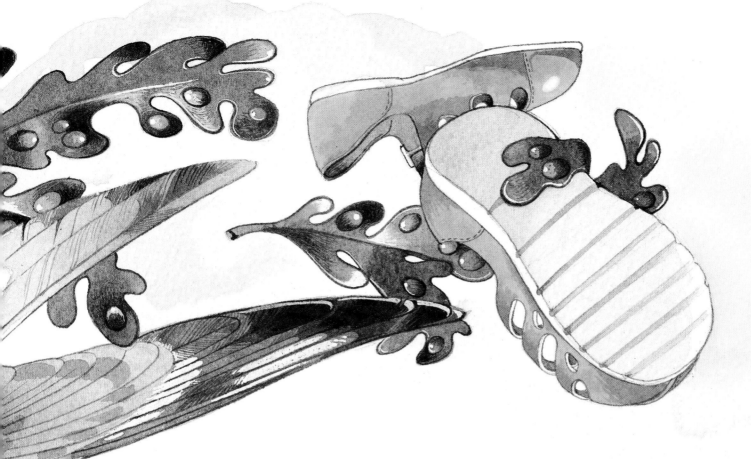

SLIP SLIPPITY SLAP!
One day when Samantha was strutting along in her sandals,
she did not see the slippery seaweed in front of her.
She fell on her face in a slimy pool.
Her sandals sailed high into the air
and sank forever in the deep blue sea.
And once again Simon was there to help her.

The other seagulls laughed and laughed
and Samantha felt embarrassed —
so embarrassed, in fact,
that she started to blush.
And her bill went red,
the rings around her eyes went red,
her legs and feet went red.

BUT THIS TIME, THAT'S HOW SHE STAYED!

"Ho, ho!" said Hector the Hermit Crab.
"You are certainly different now.
Ho, ho! Ho, ho!
I told you so."

"This is too, too terrible,"
Samantha said to Simon,
as she looked at her reflection.
"Whatever will I do?"

"Never mind," said Simon, as the two
silver gulls walked along the shore together.
"Now you are different in a very different way.
And you are even more beautiful —
the very most beautiful silver gull
in the whole wide world."
"And you, Simon," said Samantha softly,
"are very beautiful too."

And for the first time in his life,
Simon felt embarrassed —
so embarrassed, in fact,
that he started to blush.
And his bill went red,
the rings around his eyes went red,
his legs and feet went red.

AND WHAT'S MORE, THAT'S HOW THEY BOTH STAYED!

Partly True Tales — this part is true . . .

The story you have read about Samantha Seagull is make-believe. It is called a fantasy. However, part of it is true.

Silver gulls, found in Australia, really do get red feet, red bills, and red rings around their eyes when they grow up. Many birds from around the world become brightly colored as they mature. Here are a few from North America.

Vermilion flycatchers are drab brown when young, but earn their name "firehead" as they mature. They live in Mexico and the southwestern United States.

Eastern bluebirds have only a trace of color when young, but grow up to become magnificent creatures with red chests and vivid blue feathers. They can be found in Canada, Mexico, and the eastern United States.

30

Painted buntings are green and brown when young — but their coats explode with color as they mature. They live in Mexico and the southeastern United States.

Roseate spoonbills catch fire with color as they grow up — red wings, touches of yellow, a greenish beak, and a ruff of red on their chests. They can be found in Mexico and the southeastern United States.

31

Library of Congress Cataloging-in-Publication Data
Winch, Gordon, 1930-
  Samantha Seagull's sandals.

  Summary: Supported by her faithful friend Simon, a gull named Samantha
goes through a series of distinctive pairs of shoes, trying to make herself
different from all the other gulls.
  [1. Gulls--Fiction] 2. Shoes--Fiction. 3. Individuality--Fiction] I. Title.
PZ7.W7218Sam 1988 [E]   88-42923
ISBN 1-55532-909-8

North American edition first published in 1988 by

Gareth Stevens, Inc.
7317 West Green Tree Road
Milwaukee, Wisconsin 53223, USA

1 2 3 4 5 6 7 8 9 93 92 91 90 89 88